Care Bears

Christmas Cheer

By Sonia Sander   Illustrated by Rosario Pepe

ISBN-13: 978-0-439-89511-8
ISBN-10: 0-439-89511-1
CARE BEARS™© 2006 Those Characters From Cleveland, Inc.
Used under license by Scholastic Inc. All rights reserved. Published by Scholastic Inc.
SCHOLASTIC and associated logos are trademarks and/or registered trademarks of Scholastic Inc.
12 11 10 9 8 7 6 5 4 3   8 9 10/0
Printed in the U.S.A. First printing, November 2006

SCHOLASTIC INC.
New York   Toronto   London   Auckland   Sydney
Mexico City   New Delhi   Hong Kong   Buenos Aires

Funshine Bear looked out his window at the swirling snow.
He was sad because he missed the sunshine and his friends.

Christmas was only a few days away, but there wasn't a single
decoration up in Care-a-lot because of the winter storm.

Even though it was snowing, Cheer Bear didn't want
to stay inside. She decided to pay a visit to her friend.
Funshine Bear was very glad to see her.
"I've come to bring Christmas cheer!" she said.

"Let's bake Christmas cookies!" Cheer Bear said. She laid out all the ingredients they would need. "I invited our other friends to join in the fun!"

There was a knock at the door. It was Laugh-a-lot Bear and Love-a-lot
Bear! They had brought a Christmas tree and decorations.

Before long, all of their friends had arrived.
"I'm so glad you had this party," said Share Bear. "The winter
storm has kept me inside and I've missed seeing my friends."

"Baking cookies together is a great way to celebrate Christmas!" said Harmony Bear. "Do you remember how we celebrated Christmas last year?"

"I do!" answered Love-a-lot Bear. "We decorated the entire town in red ribbons and gold bells."

"That was lovely," said Love-a-lot Bear, "but I think the sweetest Christmas was when we decorated Care-a-lot in candy canes."

"It was like being in a giant candy shop!" said Champ Bear.

"But that wasn't my favorite Christmas."

"The Christmas I loved the most was the year there were presents everywhere," said Champ Bear. "I had so much fun unwrapping gifts!"

"I got everything I wished for that year," said Wish Bear. "But it's not the one I'd wish to have all over again."

"I liked the Christmas when we carved ice sculptures," said Wish Bear. "All of Care-a-lot looked like a crystal palace."

"We haven't decorated Care-a-lot at all this year,"
said Grumpy Bear. "And now it's too late to show
our Christmas cheer."

"We don't need to be outside decorating Care-a-lot to show our Christmas cheer," exclaimed Cheer Bear.

"Cheer Bear is right!" said Bedtime Bear.

"It makes me feel cheerful to be inside where it's warm and cozy!" said Bedtime Bear.

"And to be with friends," added Love-a-lot Bear.

"Sharing stories and warm memories with friends is what Christmas cheer is all about!" said Share Bear.

"Not to mention sharing cookies," joked Funshine Bear. Everyone laughed.

"This will always be our favorite Christmas!" said
Cheer Bear and Funshine Bear. "Because it has the
most Christmas cheer!"